Written By
Lawrence M. Zaccaro

Illustrated By
Ariel Friesner

Amy and the Orca

First Edition, 2018

Written, illustrated and printed in the USA

ISBN-13: 978-1984267733

ISBN-10: 1984267736

CreateSpace, a DBA of On-Demand Publishing, LLC

Amy was eight years old. She lived in a small town near the Pacific Ocean with her mom and dad, and her little brother Eric. Amy loved her family, liked playing with her friends, and she loved animals.

But her favorite thing to do was walk to the ocean with her dad.
From their special spot, they watched the sun set over the water.
They saw sea lions and bald eagles. They even saw orca whales.
Orcas were her favorite animal, but they usually weren't close enough to see well.

Amy had lots of friends, and played with them during recess and after school. She liked to read, liked school, and tried to be nice to everyone she knew.

One day, Amy's dad was listening to a song in the living room.
Some of the words in the song said, "Nights in White Satin".
Amy had only seen knights in silver armor, but the music sounded pretty to her.

In the middle of the song, Amy heard a most beautiful sound.
It soared like the voice of a magical bird.
"What's making that sound?" Amy asked her dad.
"That's a flute," he said. "A man is blowing into it to make that sound."
Amy asked "Can girls make a flute sound like that?"
"Of course they can. But anyone who plays an instrument that
well has to learn how. It's hard, like learning to read."
Amy said, "I want to play a flute!"

Andrew was a young orca whale.
Though he was as big as a pony, he was only two years old.

Andrew was part of a family of orcas called L pod.
His mother and father, two aunts,
and his older brother and sister all lived in L pod.
He sometimes teased his brother and sister.
They swam together through the cool ocean water looking for food.
Sometimes they swam near the rocky shore of Amy's favorite spot.

Andrew was very happy in L pod. He loved to sing in his orca voice.
To people, orca singing sounds like chirping or squeaking.
His parents told him not to sing,
so fish in the ocean couldn't hear them swimming.

The more his parents told him to stop singing, the sadder Andrew felt.
One day he realized that if he swam further behind, they didn't tell him to stop.
Though that made him happier, he was still sad no one wanted to hear him sing.

Ms. Lily was the music teacher at Amy's school. After classes, Ms. Lily taught Amy how to blow into her new flute to make music. At first, it didn't sound anything like the song her dad had listened to.

But Amy practiced everyday. She practiced instead of watching TV.
Sometimes she even practiced instead of walking to the ocean with her dad.

Ms. Lily taught Amy songs to play, and she was getting better. But no one seemed to like her music. Sometimes her mom and dad told her to practice in her room with the door closed.

Except for Ms. Lily, teachers and students didn't like her music either. Not even her friends. Older kids at school laughed at her when she practiced.

It made Amy sad that other people didn't like to listen.
Sometimes she didn't feel like playing her flute.

One day Amy's mom and dad asked her if she would like to have
a picnic lunch with the whole family at her special spot.
That made her happy, and she got ready to go.
"I have an idea," her dad said. "Bring your flute with you."
Amy was surprised but said, "okay."

They had a nice lunch at the special spot. When they were done eating, her dad said, "You can play as much as you want here, and as loud as you want." Amy thought that was a good idea.
She began playing a slow song. Her music seemed to sail out over the ocean.

That day, Andrew was swimming with L pod. He wasn't feeling happy. He wasn't teasing his brother or sister. He wasn't singing. Then one time when he came up to take a breath, he thought he heard something that might be singing.

"Look," said Amy's mom, "orcas! They're going to swim right by us!"
"Yay!" Said Amy. "I've never seen them this close!"
Amy played her flute a little louder, playing the prettiest song she knew.

Andrew could clearly hear this new sound. It wasn't another orca,
but it sounded friendly and nice. He got very excited.
Each time he took a breath, he swam slower and listened longer.

As they watched the other orcas of L pod swim by, Amy's mom noticed Andrew was swimming farther behind all the rest. "That little one in back," she said, "he looks like he hears you! Keep playing!"

Finally, Andrew was in front of them. He stopped completely and listened.
Then, he began singing.
Singing happily with his orca chirping and squeaking.

"He's singing back!" Amy's dad whispered excitedly. "Do you hear?"
Amy had never been so excited in her whole life! Her favorite animal
liked her flute playing! And was singing back to her!
As Amy played her pretty song, Andrew kept singing!
It made everyone so happy!
Amy's family had never seen or heard anything so wonderful!

When L pod finally swam away, Andrew made sure he remembered that spot.
Amy practiced her flute there in nice weather, keeping a close eye on the water.

Every time L pod swam by that spot, Andrew would listen.
He didn't always hear it, but when the weather was warmer,
Amy would be there almost every time, happily playing her flute.

Amy loved playing her flute after that. She worked hard at practicing.
She played every year in school, and was in the high school orchestra.
None of the kids ever laughed at her then. Everyone loved to hear her play.
She went to a special college to learn to play the flute much better.

The orcas in L pod didn't mind that Andrew stopped to sing.
Whenever they had enough food and could rest, they all stopped and sang too!
When Amy went to college, Andrew was full grown and still in L pod.

For years to come, on days Amy played in their special spot,
Andrew and all of L pod stopped and sang along with her flute.
Their beautiful music together filled the land and water around them all.

The End

About the Author

Lawrence M. Zaccaro lives in Connecticut. After a career as a research scientist, he has completed numerous creative endeavors. He has written a novel, movie screenplays, and created an educational game called Wordplay. Amy and the Orca is his first children's book. Mr. Zaccaro may be reached at zaccarolarry@gmail.com.

About the Artist

Ariel Friesner is a freelance artist from Chicago, IL. This is the fifth children's book she has had the pleasure of illustrating! Besides drawing, Ariel enjoys cooking and streaming her artwork on Twitch. You can contact Ariel via :
Arielfriesner@gmail.com - www.Instagram.com/Arielarto - Twitch.tv/Ariellarto

Made in the USA
Coppell, TX
03 December 2021